MY BROTHER IS A

ROBOT

BOOK 4

THE FIGHT

AMANDA RONAN

The Fight
My Brother is a Robot #4

Copyright © 2016

Published by Scobre Educational

Written by Amanda Ronan

Printed in the United States of America.

Scobre Educational
2255 Calle Clara
La Jolla, CA 92037

Scobre Operations & Administration
42982 Osgood Road
Fremont, CA 94539

www.scobre.com
info@scobre.com

Scobre Educational publications may be purchased for educational, business, or sales promotional use.

Cover and layout design by Nicole Ramsay
Copyedited by Kristin Russo

ISBN: 978-1-62920-504-5 (Library Bound)
ISBN: 978-1-62920-503-8 (eBook)

For Mom and Dad, who have always believed in me.

CHAPTER 1

I HELD MY HAND OVER MY EYES, PROTECTING THEM FROM THE SUN, and squinted at the lake. "Do you see him?" I asked my mom, who was sitting in a plastic chair next to me.

She peered over the top of her book and shook her head. "No, he's probably just admiring the underwater scenery."

"But he's been under for awhile. How can he hold his breath that long?" I asked, sitting up straighter, feeling worried that my brother Cyrus might be in trouble under the water.

My dad walked up behind me and put his hand on my shoulder. "Shawn, he doesn't have lungs. He's not holding his breath."

"Oh, yeah," I said, reminded suddenly that despite his recent adoption, my brother Cyrus was actually a robot.

My mom was a mechanical engineer and Cyrus was her latest project. He was the most human-like robot that had ever been created. In fact, he was so human-like that he looked just like me. No kidding. We're nearly identical twins on the outside. Mom brought Cyrus home about six months ago to improve his emotional processing skills. At first he caused a lot of trouble around the house. His alarms would go off in the middle of the night and it drove my dad crazy. Then I asked Cyrus for help with my math homework, but really, I tricked him into doing it all for me. I got caught cheating and kicked off the basketball team. My dad was furious, but as much as he blamed me, he also blamed Cyrus. He was so upset about all the trouble that Cyrus brought that he wanted him out of our lives. But, instead of leaving, Cyrus won my dad over by building him a new and improved kitchen. Cyrus found out my dad loved to cook and had even traveled around the world learning how to make great food. When the kitchen renovation took longer than expected, my dad and Cyrus worked on rebuilding it together and they have been close ever since.

A few months ago, I got back on the basketball team, but still had to work hard to keep my grades up. Cyrus agreed to pretend to be me at a game so I could finish my homework. One of Mom's coworkers, Dr. Geno, found out about our switch and informed everyone in the community. He made the parents of the kids at school anxious that robots would start doing lots of bad things and we'd never know because they're so human-like. The lab nearly shut down Mom's project and discontinued Cyrus, but my friends and I started a social media campaign to help his image. After a video of Cyrus rescuing a kid who got his hand stuck inside a skee-ball machine went viral, the lab offered to let Mom and Dad officially adopt Cyrus. After all that drama, school finally ended and our family decided to get away from town for a while and recover from all the ups and downs. So, we came to my grandparents' cabin on the lake.

Cyrus had been underwater for at least ten minutes when I finally stood up and marched to the water's edge. "I'm going to go find him," I called over my shoulder.

"When you do, tell him I need him to help light the oven. The pilot light went out," Dad called from behind his tablet. He'd spent the whole vacation playing solitaire and watching videos of cute dogs. I think he was missing our basset hound, Scooter, who was staying with my best friend, James, while we were away.

I pulled the plastic mask over my eyes and stuck

the snorkel in my mouth. I walked through the water until it got deep enough to float. Then, I stuck my head under and started paddling toward the sand dunes where Cyrus had last come ashore.

Adopting Cyrus took a while because the courts weren't sure how to handle a robot becoming part of a human family. Eventually, though, everything worked out, and to celebrate, we wanted to do something really special for Cyrus. It was tough shopping for a robot that had a super-computer mind and could access all the online information in the world with just a quick search of his databases. Because we knew we'd take a trip the lake, Mom worked with the lab to design Cyrus a completely leak-proof, full-body wet suit that would allow him to swim without compromising his circuitry. At first he'd been worried about whether the suit would really work. But once he trusted it and went for his first swim, he was impossible to get out of the water.

The lake water was a little murky, though I could see some fish swim by on my way to the dunes. Unlike Cyrus, I didn't love spending so much time in the water. When I was younger, we'd come up here with my grandparents and one time I stepped on a snake in the water. It was a few years before I would even go close to the shoreline after that.

Happy to reach the sand dunes, I took a careful step out of the water. I hadn't seen any sign of Cyrus on my swim. I sat on the sand and started to toss a few rocks into the water. I thought he'd see or hear the pebbles and know I was trying to contact him. I waited a few minutes and nothing happened. "Cyrus!" I yelled at the top of my lungs, which was okay, because our nearest neighbors were miles away. But still I got no response.

I looked back toward the shore and saw that both of my parents were gone from their beach chairs. It reminded me that in a few more days, we'd pack up and drive home. Cyrus and I started sixth grade in a week. No more elementary school, we were officially middle schoolers. I couldn't wait. The basketball team would be better, the classes would be more interesting, and the girls would be cuter.

"This is crazy," I said to myself. Cyrus could find his way home with his eyes closed. My stomach gurgled a little. It had to be close to suppertime.

I put my mask back on and stuck my snorkel back in my mouth. I swam slowly back to shore, still keeping an eye out for Cyrus. When I hit the beach, I dropped my stuff on my chair and climbed the stone path that led to the house. I could smell dinner cooking and hear my parents laughing. I could also hear Cyrus. I jogged up the last few steps and rounded the corner. Mom, Dad, and Cyrus were sitting at the patio table.

"Oh! Shawn! Just in time." My mom smiled.

I put my hands on my hips and glared at Cyrus. "Where have you been? I went out looking for you."

Cyrus pointed to the plates in front of my parents. "I caught a fish for dinner."

"And he removed the scales, deboned it, filleted it, and cooked it perfectly after relighting the stove," my dad said, beaming, and then he reached over and ruffled Cyrus's hair.

I rolled my eyes. "The perfect son." I loved my brother, but it was hard feeling like I couldn't do things as well as him. He had almost no flaws, and I had plenty.

My mom patted the seat next to her. "One of two perfect sons," she said, smiling. "One of two perfect sixth graders. Oh my goodness. Where has the time gone?"

I looked down at my plate and had to hand it to Cyrus: the fish looked amazing. It wasn't easy being a human kid when you had a robot brother, but at least the perks could be tasty.

CHAPTER 2

As we waited for the bus, my best friend James asked about the trip to the lake. When I told him it was fine, he turned to Cyrus to ask the same question. Cyrus droned on and on about the trip. He told James that swimming was like nothing he'd ever experienced before. I wondered how the two of them could be so calm on the first day of school.

I'd woken up extra early that morning. I was too nervous to sleep in. Scooter, who'd been curled up on the end of my bed, was not a morning dog, so he barely stirred as I got dressed. Just like in elementary school, we had to wear a uniform. But in middle school we had our choice of shirt colors—white, blue, gray, or red. It was a tough choice for the first day. I wondered what the older kids would wear. I decided on a white shirt because it matched my brand new white on white basketball sneakers.

"I think I hear the bus," I said, craning my neck to see around the big oak trees that lined our street.

"I think that's the garbage truck," Cyrus said. "It's only seven fifteen. The bus is scheduled to be here at seven twenty-five."

James punched my shoulder jokingly. "What are you so nervous about, Shawn? We got this. Dolores Huerta Middle School won't know what hit them."

Cyrus tilted his head to one side and asked, "Why are you going to hit the school?"

James looked at me as if to ask if my brother was serious until Cyrus burst out laughing, "Just kidding!

You really thought I didn't understand your use of figurative language. But I did."

James grinned and shook his head, "The point of a joke, Cy, is that you don't have to explain it. We'll keep working on that."

I shielded my eyes from the rising sun and pointed. "There's the bus!" I looked at my watch and said, "A whole five minutes early." I bit my lips nervously as the orange-yellow bus stopped at the corner. I could see through the windows that there were already a bunch of kids on the bus. Hopefully James, Cyrus, and I would find an empty seat to share. As I started walking toward the open bus door behind Cyrus, my foot slipped off the curb.

Splash! I looked down already knowing what I'd see. The extra rainy summer had left puddles and mud pits all over our neighborhood. The brand new, all white shoe on my left foot was now stuck in the mud. My foot had slipped out of my shoe as I tried to free myself from the muck. "Argh," I cried as I leaned over to grab my sneaker.

"Come on, kid, we can't be late on the first day!" I heard the bus driver shout out the door.

I was so embarrassed I felt like I should turn around and go home rather than face the bus full of kids. "Coming!" I called and tried to shake off as much mud from my shoe as possible. At least I knew James and Cyrus would save me a spot, so I could slide my sneaker on once I sat down.

As I climbed the stairs and looked around, though, I didn't see Cyrus saving me a seat. I saw him high-fiving a bunch of older kids who were asking him about his robot powers. I finally made eye contact with James, who waved me over.

I sat down quickly and slid my foot in my shoe. "I can't believe I just ruined my new sneakers. This day can't get any worse."

James nodded over at Cyrus. "Actually, it probably

can. Looks like Cyrus is already best friends with the eighth graders, making you significantly uncooler than your robot brother."

I looked over at James. "Thanks. That helps a lot," I said sarcastically.

"No problem, buddy," James laughed, and he chatted my ear off for the rest of the fifteen minute ride to school.

The morning passed quickly and by lunch time I was pretty sure I'd be able to find my away around. My classes seemed like they were going to be tough. I'd done extra work over the summer to keep my math skills fresh, so I hoped that would help me stay on top of things this year.

I'd managed to wipe most of the mud off my shoe when we got to school, but some of it was caked into the seams. I wasn't sure it would ever get clean.

Cyrus and I didn't have any of the same morning

classes, but we'd be together in two classes in the afternoon. Since all the sixth graders had lunch at the same time, I knew I'd see him when I walked into the cafeteria. I was curious about how his day was going. By the way the older kids had reacted to him on the bus, I figured he'd be tired of being recognized as the new robot kid.

"Hey," I said, sitting at a table with Jensen, Colton, and Demarcus, from my elementary school's basketball team. I tossed my lunch bag onto the table and Jensen snickered.

"You've got to start buying lunch at the snack bar, man. No one in middle school brings a packed lunch," Jensen said, pointing up to the long line by the salad bar. "You can get pizza slices, French fries, and gigantic chocolate chip cookies!"

My mouth watered just thinking about all the junk food. I knew I wouldn't find anything like that when I emptied my bag on the table. My dad and

Cyrus continued to enjoy their kitchen renovation by making weird, gourmet foods for dinner and, just like last year, I ended up with leftovers for lunch. On that first day of middle school, I had a bagel covered with smoked salmon, chive cream cheese, and arugula. Oh, and a kale salad with citrus salad dressing on the side. "Maybe I can convince my mom to give me lunch money. Or maybe Cyrus will give me some of his money from the lab," I said, drooling.

"Nope," Cyrus said appearing out of nowhere and sitting down next to me. He was returning from the snack bar with James, who was carrying four paper plates with pizza slices.

I eyed James, who was not watching where he was going. He was trying to wave hello to all our old classmates. I saw one of his plates slipping out of his hand, so I leaned forward to try and catch it. Instead of grabbing the plate, James managed to turn at the last second and run smack into me. All four slices of pizza smooshed against my chest. Besides the burning sensation of hot pizza seeping through the shirt, I knew sauce and cheese was covering me from my neck to my belt.

All the guys at the table laughed loudly. I grumbled a little to myself as I dabbed at the shirt with a napkin. When the laughter got louder, I looked up and saw Cyrus pretending to be me. He replayed the pizza spill in slow motion and perfected my horrified facial expressions.

"Ha!" Demarcus laughed. "It's funny because they're identical. Cyrus looks just like Shawn!"

The guys kept asking Cyrus to do his impression again and again. And every time they asked, he made it even more exaggerated and over the top. I felt myself get hot as I watched him mocking me. My anger was bubbling in my chest. I stood and slammed my fists on the table.

"Shawn, man, it's fine. Just go to the office and get

a new shirt," I heard James call after me as I huffed out of the cafeteria.

And it would have been fine if lunch wasn't almost over and if the eighth graders weren't already lined up outside the cafeteria waiting to come in. As I walked by them, I tried not to make eye contact, hoping that if I acted like I didn't care, they wouldn't say anything.

But instead, the comments came flying out so fast my head spun. "What's a matter, baby can't eat his pizza?" "Did you forget where your mouth was, kid?" "Didn't your parents teach you how to chew your food?"

I picked up speed and ran to the bathroom. I tried dabbing at the shirt, but it was no use. The stains would never come out. I didn't have time to make it to the office to get a new shirt before my next class, so I spent the rest of the day smelling like pizza and looking like a slob. Every time we passed to new classes, someone made a comment. By the time the end of the day bell rang, I was sure middle school would not be the best three years of my life.

CHAPTER 3

THE NEXT DAY I WORE MY OLD BLACK SNEAKERS AND A BLACK shirt. That way, if I got dirty, it wouldn't be so obvious.

Cyrus didn't apologize for making fun of me, so I ignored him at home. He tried talking to me, but I just said I was busy with homework and closed my bedroom door.

I made it through the first few weeks without embarrassing myself too much, but people don't forget first impressions and it seemed like I was doomed to be known as "Pizza Boy" forever. Cyrus, on the other hand, was gaining popularity. The older kids thought Cyrus was so smart and so interesting. They were always inviting him to sit with them on the bus and to hang out with them during assemblies. He seemed to be making friends much faster than he had last year.

Basketball tryouts were coming up, so I put Cyrus out of my mind and focused on practicing whenever I could. The weekend before tryouts I was outside shooting hoops at the end of my driveway. My dad came out and sat on the curb. He watched as I practiced my three-point shot from every angle. Finally he said, "Your technique is looking really good Shawn. Your practice is really paying off."

I nodded a thank you, but didn't take my eyes off the net.

"Do you know where your brother went?" Dad asked, standing and holding his hands out asking for the ball.

I shook my head, feeling out of breath, and bounced the ball over to him.

"He said he was going to play soccer with some friends. Who has he been hanging out with?" My dad was dribbling slowly as he spoke.

I shrugged and tapped the ball out of his hands, ran toward the net, and tossed the ball in. "I don't know, Dad. Cyrus and I haven't really been hanging out since school started. I usually just see James and the other guys. Cyrus has been hanging out with the older kids."

Dad walked back toward the house and then stopped and turned around. "Hey, Shawn, give your brother a break sometimes, okay? Just because he's a super computer doesn't mean he's always going to make super smart decisions."

I dribbled the ball as I watched him go. Why was Dad worrying about Cyrus? He was turning into a popular super star at school and leaving me behind. I didn't care what Cyrus did. I had to focus on my game.

"Hey, Shawn," a voice said from behind my locker.

I closed the cool metal door slightly and came face to face with Chantal Baxter, the girl I'd had a crush on since kindergarten. She'd always been friendly, but I don't think we'd ever had an actual one on one conversation.

"Oh." My voice squeaked. I coughed to clear my throat. "Oh, hey, Chantal. How's it going?" Man, I was smooth.

She smiled and curled a strand of dark brown hair around her finger as she leaned against the locker near mine. "It's really good. How are you liking middle school so far?"

Was this really happening? I thought I should pinch myself to make sure I wasn't imagining it. "Yeah, it's great. Really cool. What about you?"

"I love it. I just made the cheerleading squad last

week, so I'll be seeing you at the games." She held her science book in one hand.

"Well, I haven't made the team yet. Tryouts are after school." I smiled and started to walk toward the science lab with her.

She laughed and put her hand on my shoulder and said, "Of course you'll make it! You were the best player on the team last year."

I felt warm and I ducked my head to make sure she couldn't see me blushing. "Yeah, when I wasn't kicked off the team or having Cyrus pretend to be me." I hoped joking would make me feel less shy.

"Speaking of Cyrus," Chantal said, dropping her book on the table in the lab and taking the seat next to mine. "How's he doing this year? He seems so different, so much more human."

I sighed. "He's fine. Making new friends, finding new interests. It's good for him to try new things. It helps him gather more information for his databases."

Chantal's green eyes sparkled and she laughed shyly, "Does he, um, does he have a girlfriend?"

I chuckled, "Uh, no. Cyrus doesn't even know what a girl is." I saw her face fall with disappointment, "Why, do you . . . do you like Cyrus? Like, *like*-like him?"

"No," Chantal rushed to say quickly and then hung her head. "Okay, yeah. I do. Ever since last year when we were in math class together. There's just something so, I don't know, cool about him. Anyway, could you maybe find out if he likes me?"

I stared at her and wanted to say, "No. Absolutely not. You shouldn't like my brother, who's a robot by the way. You should like me." Instead, I said through a clenched jaw, "Yeah. Sure."

Chantal reached over and hugged me. "You're the best! Thank you!"

When she walked away I could still feel where she hugged me and I couldn't stop smiling. But then

Cyrus walked into the room, flanked by some of his new buddies. He slid in the seat where Chantal had just been sitting and said, "Hey."

I frowned and looked away from him. Just because we were brothers didn't mean we had to be best friends.

CHAPTER 4

"**A**LRIGHT, I WANT TO SEE COLE, WALKER, JAMIL, Hendricks, and Fletcher versus Harlow, McClure, Basile, Rowan, and Jackson," called out Coach Stanley.

We'd started tryouts with basic drills and individual skill work. After thirty minutes of that, the coach wanted to see us scrimmage. He was looking to see how we played as a team, how we worked with other people, and how we played under pressure.

There were ten sixth graders, twenty seventh

graders, and twenty-five eighth graders at tryouts. I felt like I held my own compared to the older guys. I definitely messed up and missed a few shots, but overall I tried my best. The hours of practice I'd been putting in felt like they were paying off.

I stood at center court facing Bill Harlow during the tip-off. Before the whistle blew, he smirked at me. "Let's see what you got, Pizza Boy. Hope you play with more coordination than you eat."

I closed my eyes and bit the inside of my cheek to get my anger under control. But in the second that it took for me to regain my composure, the coach had blown the whistle and Harlow had tapped the ball over my head to his teammates. I hadn't even jumped for the ball. I knew how bad that must have looked. The disappointment stayed with me for the next eight minutes while we played a quarter.

When my turn was over, I sat on the bench and watched the rest of the groups cycle onto the court and play. I just shook my head every time I thought of my mistake. Hopefully, the coach would look past it and remember the good work I did earlier that afternoon.

At the end of tryouts, the coach asked everyone to wait for a few minutes while he typed up the list of names of people who had made the team. Those fifteen minutes felt like a decade. When he finally posted the list, everyone gathered around to look. Not many sixth graders made it—James and Colton did. I smiled at them from my spot in line. As the coach approached where I was standing, he smiled and said, "Sorry, Cole." I didn't even bother getting closer to the list. I just turned around and went to the locker room.

I wanted to cry. But I knew I had to hold it together. I couldn't be known as a crybaby Pizza Boy.

As we rode home on the late bus, James tried to make me feel better. "You'll get another shot next year. Just hold on until then. You're too good to give up, Shawn."

I shrugged and looked around for Cyrus. He was sitting in the back of the bus with an earbud stuck in one ear. He was nodding his head in time to music. Since when did Cyrus listen to music? The guys around him were hollering and acting goofy. I shook my head in confusion. I barely even recognized my brother, which was weird, considering we were identical twins.

When my mom asked how our days were over dinner, I looked sadly at my plate and whispered, "I didn't make the basketball team."

"I made the soccer team!" Cyrus said loudly at the same time.

I looked up sharply, "You what?!"

Cyrus was sitting across from me, smiling from ear to ear, "I made the soccer team. I'm the starting center midfielder."

My parents both reached over to hug him. "Congratulations, Cyrus!" my mom exclaimed.

"My boy!" My dad grinned excitedly. Then he looked over at me. "And what about you, Shawn? How were basketball tryouts?"

I slammed my hands on the table as I stood, flinging my fork in the air. "I said I didn't make the team," I shouted and stormed out of the room. I had to step over Scooter who rushed over to investigate any food particles left on my fallen fork.

I stayed in my room all night and ignored my family's pitying looks over breakfast. On the bus, I listened to James babble on about some project he was working on in history class. When we got to school, I didn't want to be around anybody, so I hurried to the bathroom. I stared at my reflection in the mirror and frowned. Why was I failing so badly at middle school? I struggled to keep up with my classes, didn't make the basketball team, and agreed to help the girl of my dreams date my brother, who wasn't even my friend anymore!

I heard the door open and guys laughing, so I ducked into the stall in the corner. I didn't want to get caught staring at myself in the mirror.

"So you're sure you won't consider using your robot smarts and titanium legs to help us win? I mean, you do want to win, don't you?" I peeked through the crack in the door and saw Cyrus with Jeff and Rodney, two of the eighth graders on the soccer team. Jeff was facing Cyrus waiting for an answer.

Cyrus nodded. "I do want to win, but I want to do it fairly. After the whole basketball switch last year, I'm lucky the school will even let me play sports. The agreement was that I set my controls to normal human level abilities. Sorry, guys."

"What if you accidentally forget to reset your controls?" Rodney asked, looking proud of himself for coming up with the ridiculous idea.

"Well then, that wouldn't be an accident. Like I said,

I'll play like everyone else. We'll still win. I'm that good," Cyrus smiled and walked out of the bathroom.

"Haha, so that robot kid's a trip, huh?" I heard Rodney say.

"Yeah, man, he's going to help us win the soccer championship this year," Jeff said, looking in his backpack. "And while he's at it, he's going to help us ace our science class." He held out what looked like homework and said, "He already gave me all the answers on the bus."

Rodney grabbed at the paper. "For real? I need to copy that." While he was writing the answers on his own paper, he asked, "How are we going to convince him to use his bionic powers?"

Jeff smirked. "I'm working on a plan. You know his brother?"

Rodney snorted, "Pizza Boy? How are those two even related? Cyrus is so cool and Pizza Boy is such a loser."

I bit down on the inside of my cheek to keep from saying anything. I was trying not to breathe too loudly so they wouldn't know I was listening.

"They're not actually related, stupid. Cyrus is a robot, so he can't actually be related to a human. Anyway, though, Cyrus would do anything for his brother. He talks about him all the time. I think if we can get Pizza Boy to convince Cyrus to program himself to be unstoppable at the game, he'd do it."

The two boys high-fived and left the bathroom. I let myself out of the stall and unclenched my fists. I needed to find Cyrus immediately.

CHAPTER 5

AS I RAN DOWN TO THE HALLWAY LOOKING FOR CYRUS, I wondered what I was going to say to him. Maybe we could come up with a plan to get back at those eighth graders for trying to use Cyrus to win. It would be like old times, with the two of us scheming together.

When I got closer to Cyrus's locker, I heard a familiar giggle. Chantal was standing there laughing at something Cyrus said like it was the funniest thing in the world. I stopped at the water fountain and pretended to get a drink to listen to what they were saying.

"I like your fingernail polish," Cyrus said, taking Chantal's hand in his. "It complements your skin tone."

Chantal blushed and smiled at Cyrus. "You are so sweet."

Cyrus nodded. "I'm programmed that way."

Chantal laughed and swatted at Cyrus's shoulder in a flirtatious way. "So, Cyrus, I was wondering . . . " She took a deep breath and I could tell she was about to ask him out. I couldn't let that happen. Something came over me in that moment. All the anger I'd felt about Cyrus laughing at me, the torment about being called "Pizza Boy," not making the basketball team, Cyrus's popularity, Chantal's crush on Cyrus, the soccer guys wanting to use me to get to Cyrus . . . It was all too much.

"Hi, Chantal. I need to talk to my brother," I interrupted, and grabbed Cyrus by the shoulder.

He shrugged me off. "Shawn, we're talking right now. I'll see you later." Cyrus turned back to Chantal, "Sorry, you were saying something?"

"No," I said angrily, "we need to talk right now." I grabbed him again, much harder this time and his shoulder slammed against the lockers behind him.

Cyrus's eyes widened and I could tell he was trying to make sense of what was happening, "Are you trying to fight with me?" He asked like he couldn't believe it.

I crossed my arms in front of my chest. "So what if I am?"

Cyrus looked confused. "But why? What did I do?"

I pushed his chest and he fell back again. "You know what you did. You've been a jerk for weeks now and even though I didn't have to, I came over here to tell you that the older kids on the soccer team are just using you to win. But noooooo . . . you're too busy flirting with the girl I've liked forever to even *listen* to me!"

Cyrus stood upright and lowered his voice, "Shawn, my environmental sensors are telling me that your heart rate and blood pressure are going through the roof. You need to take a few deep breaths and regulate your body. Then we'll talk." He started to turn away from me and I lost it. Having a robot for a brother could be really cool sometimes. He could hack into video games and get cheat codes to make it easier to win. He gave good pointers on my basketball game, suggesting better angles for my shot release. But right now, having him tell me to regulate my vital signs was not a cool moment in our brotherly history.

I grabbed Cyrus around the neck to turn him back around.

"Shawn! What are you doing?" Chantal had been watching the whole argument unfold between me and Cyrus. But now that she saw me trying actually harm him, she couldn't stay quiet. "Jenny, go get a teacher," she called to her friend walking by.

Cyrus was pushing against me to free himself from the headlock. "You're being crazy right now. Let me go before you get in trouble." He pushed a little harder and I had to take a few steps backwards. Right then, Mr. Jennings, the vice principal, came around the corner.

After seeing the group of students circling us and watching the fight, he cleared his throat loudly and bellowed, "Just what is going on here? Mr. Cole and, er, Mr. Cole, go to my office right now."

I grabbed my backpack. "Fine."

Cyrus followed behind me shaking his head, still confused by what had just happened.

"Shawn, Cyrus? Come on in." Ms. Roberts, the school counselor, opened her office door. Mr. Jennings sent us to see her when we got to the office because he had a parent meeting to attend. He thought we needed counseling more than we needed discipline, which is what he said before he left.

"So, what happened?" the counselor asked, folding her hands across her desk. There were posters with inspirational sayings on them all over her office. I snickered as I read them, thinking they were pretty corny.

"He started it!" both Cyrus and I said at the same time. We looked at each other and laughed a little.

"Well, there. Now you're laughing together. Does this mean your anger has passed?" she asked, tilting her head.

Cyrus shrugged. "I didn't have any anger. My system regulates itself so that I don't have upswings of emotions. This is coming from Shawn."

Ms. Roberts looked at me. "Is that true, Shawn? Did you start this?"

I exhaled loudly and slumped in my chair. "I guess."

"Why?" she asked.

I shrugged. I didn't need therapy. I needed my brother to have my back and not be such a jerk.

"Use your words, Shawn," Cyrus said leaning over. I could tell by the small smile on his lips that he was trying to be funny.

"Yeah, I'm angry," I admitted.

"About what?" Ms. Roberts leaned forward eagerly.

"I dunno. I didn't make the basketball team because one of the guys distracted me by calling me names. Everyday people call me 'Pizza Boy" because I spilled pizza on me the first day of school and everybody laughed, even Cyrus, and he never said he was sorry. Then he got new friends and made the soccer team and made everyone think he was so cool and just forgot about me. Then Chantal decided that she liked him and was going to ask him out—"

Cyrus leaned forward again. "She was?"

I nodded. "She asked me to find out if you liked her."

"You never said anything," Cyrus pointed out.

"Right, because *I* like her. So I wasn't going to let *you* like her," I explained.

Cyrus thought about this and then laughed, "Were we fighting over a girl? This is just like the movies. I think this experience made me even *more* like a human."

I rolled my eyes. "Stop teasing."

"Boys, may I interject?" Ms. Roberts asked.

We both nodded.

"You two obviously care about each other. Shawn, you've been angry and upset because you feel betrayed by your brother. Also, being in a new environment where you don't have the social status you had in elementary school has been difficult for you. Cyrus, you've been busy trying to have new human-like experiences that you forgot to think about your primary relationships. Does this sound right?"

Cyrus and I looked at each other.

"Yeah," I finally said. "I guess I just didn't know

what to do with everything I was feeling, so trying to hurt Cyrus was the only thing I could come up with."

"You're lucky he didn't fight back," Ms. Roberts said seriously. "I have the feeling if he had, you would be in serious pain right now."

I let that thought sink in. Trying to fight a robot was a seriously stupid move on my part.

Cyrus looked pleased. "It's true. I am a black belt in seven different martial arts, thanks to downloadable videos."

Everyone laughed. Ms. Roberts made us apologize and promise to be nicer to each other. Then she gave us hall passes and sent us back to class.

In the hallway, Cyrus put his hand on my shoulder. "Seriously, though, Shawn. I'm sorry I've been ignoring you. I was trying to develop my own life, but that should have still included you."

I smiled. "Thanks, bro. And I'm sorry I got so angry and tried to hurt you."

"Just hang in there," Cyrus smiled.

I laughed at the reference to the poster of the kitten hanging in the tree in Ms. Robert's office.

"Hey Cyrus, don't make excuses, make improvements," I said, quoting another poster.

He laughed, "No one can do everything, but everyone can do something."

"Genius is one percent inspiration and ninety-nine percent perspiration," I said.

Cyrus frowned. "Not true. I'm a genius and I don't perspire."

I swatted his shoulder. "You're so weird."

He shrugged. "I learned it from you. And just so you know, I knew those guys were using me. And to pay them back I gave them all the wrong answers on their science homework."

Now *that* was the brother I'd been missing.